Hey Jack! Books

First American Edition 2021
Kane Miller, A Division of EDC Publishing
Original Title: Hey Jack: The Party Invite
Text Copyright © 2014 Sally Rippin
Illustration Copyright © 2014 Stephanie Spartels
Logo and Design Copyright © 2014 Hardie Grant Children's Publishing
First published in Australia by Hardie Grant Children's Publishing
All rights reserved, including the rights of reproduction
in whole or in part in any form.

For information contact:
Kane Miller, A Division of EDC Publishing
5402 S 122nd E Ave, Tulsa, OK 74146
www.kanemiller.com
www.myubam.com
Library of Congress Control Number: 2021934742
Printed and bound in the United States of America
1 2 3 4 5 6 7 8 9 10
ISBN: 978-1-68464-308-0

The Party Invite

By Sally Rippin

Illustrated by Stephanie Spartels

Kane Miller
A DIVISION OF EDC PUBLISHING

Chapter One

This is Jack. Today Jack is in a hurt mood. He is feeling hurt because he hasn't been invited to Rebecca's birthday party.

Jack's best friend, Billie, is invited to the party. She showed Jack her invitation after school today. Rebecca is having a sleepover party. It sounds like lots of fun.

Jack feels cross that he wasn't invited. Rebecca is *his* friend, too!

He even feels cross with
Billie for showing him
the invitation.

When he saw it he ran all the way back to his house through the hole in the back fence.

Now he is lying on his bed feeling **mad** and **bad**, but mostly **sad**.

He begins to worry.

Why didn't she invite me? he wonders.

4

I invited her to my party. Maybe she doesn't like me anymore? Maybe nobody likes me?

Jack imagines everyone in his class having fun at Rebecca's party without him. He feels more **miserable** than ever.

The next day at school, Jack and Billie walk past Rebecca in the playground.

She is standing with a group of girls from their class. They are talking and laughing together.

"Hey, Jack! Hey, Billie!" Rebecca calls when she sees them.

Billie stops to wave. But Jack looks away and pretends he didn't hear.

He walks straight past the girls into the school building. Billie skips to catch up with him.

"Hey, Jack, what's up?" Billie asks. "You've been acting **weird** all morning. Didn't you hear Rebecca say hello?"

Jack frowns and shakes his head. Billie looks at him strangely. Billie and Jack have known each other forever.

Billie knows Jack better than anyone in the world. Except maybe Scraps.

It is very hard for Jack to hide how he feels from Billie.

Jack scrunches up his face.

"You wouldn't understand,"
he says grumpily.

"Everyone likes *you*."

"What are you talking
about?" Billie says.

Jack thinks about telling
Billie how he feels.

Doing this usually makes
him feel better.

But then he remembers
that Billie was one of
the people invited to
Rebecca's party.

*How can she go to Rebecca's
party without me?* he
thinks, feeling **cross** all
over again.

"It's nothing!" he says,
and pushes past Billie
into the classroom.

13

But as soon as he sits down he feels bad for being cross with Billie. She hasn't really done anything wrong.

14

Billie walks into the classroom and **glares** at Jack. Then she sits down at a desk on the other side of the room. Jack slumps down in his chair.

Now even Billie doesn't want to be my friend, he thinks glumly. *This is the worst day ever.*

Chapter Two

Jack sits by himself
during show-and-tell.
He sits by himself during
math. Even during
library time, he sits by

himself. Jack finds a place on his own in the corner and opens his library book.

Instead of reading though, Jack looks around at everyone in his class. They are all having **fun** without him. Sometimes they look up and see him looking at them.

Then they whisper to
each other and look away.

I knew it! Jack thinks. *Everyone in the class is going to Rebecca's party except me. Nobody likes me.*

He feels like he has a small black cloud in his chest as they walk back to class from the library.

When the bell goes for recess, Jack packs up his things very slowly.

"You coming to play soccer?" Billie says. She hangs around in the doorway.

"Nah," says Jack. "I don't feel like it today."

Billie frowns. "But we need you, Jack!" she says. "Our team will be one player short otherwise."

Jack frowns. *They don't really want me to play,* he thinks. *Billie is just saying that.*

"I told you," he says

grumpily. "I don't feel

like playing today, OK?"

Billie stares at Jack.

"I don't know what's

wrong with you today,"

she says. "But you are

acting very strangely."

"Nothing's wrong,"

Jack says crossly.

"Can't I have one day off from soccer? I don't always have to do what you tell me!"

Jack looks at Billie's face.
He can see he has hurt
her feelings. He feels bad.

But his feelings have
been hurt too!

Billie **frowns** at Jack
one more time, then runs
out of the classroom.

Jack sits all alone in the
classroom with the small
black cloud in his chest.

Part of him wants to run
after Billie and say sorry.
Then he could join the
soccer game.

But another part of him isn't quite ready to let go of that cross feeling inside him.

Chapter Three

Jack is still sitting in
the classroom when
Rebecca walks in a few
minutes later. Her mom
is walking behind her.

They are each carrying a big plastic container. They put them down on the teacher's desk.

Jack looks at them in surprise. He didn't expect to see Rebecca right now. He feels all **jumbled up** inside. He is happy to see his friend, but he is still feeling cross, too.

"Hey, Jack!" Rebecca says.

"Hey, Rebecca," Jack
mumbles. "What's that?"
He points to the plastic
containers.

"Cupcakes," says Rebecca.

"It's my birthday today!"

"Oh, right," says Jack.

"Happy birthday."

Then he remembers
Billie's invitation and
feels upset all over again.

"That's right," he says,
grumpily. "Your party is
this weekend, isn't it?"

"Yeah," Rebecca says.

"I wanted to have a

sleepover so Mom said

I could only invite four

people. It was *so* hard to

decide who to invite!"

"Really? Just four?"

says Jack. He feels a

fizzle in his tummy.

So it's not just me who wasn't invited! he thinks.

Rebecca nods. "I was **worried** that some of my friends might feel left out," she says, biting her lip.

She pauses. "Jack, are you mad at me? I mean, we're still friends, right?"

The little black cloud in Jack's chest feels lighter and lighter.

He begins to giggle.
He suddenly feels very
silly that he got so
upset about the party
invitation.

"Of course we're still friends, Rebecca!" he says, laughing. "I know you can't always invite *everyone*!"

"Phew!" says Rebecca. "I'm glad you understand, Jack. I was worried you might be **cross** with me! Especially when you didn't wave to me in the playground this morning."

"Nah," says Jack. He feels a little embarrassed.

He puts his arm around Rebecca's shoulder.

"I was grumpy about something. But I feel better now."

"Hey, can you help me hand out the cupcakes before the bell goes?" Rebecca asks.

"Sure!" says Jack. "I'd love to help!"

Jack and Rebecca pick up a container each.

Just then Jack remembers something.

He is glad he has made up with Rebecca. But now he needs to make up with someone else as well. He knows just what he has to do.

He finds the **best** cupcake in the container.

"Come on!" he says to Rebecca, grinning. "I know who will *love* one of these! And if we hurry, we might be in time to catch the end of the soccer game, too."

Hey Jack! The Crazy Cousins
By Sally Rippin

Hey Jack! The Scary Solo
By Sally Rippin

Hey Jack! The Winning Goal
By Sally Rippin

Hey Jack! The Robot Blues
By Sally Rippin

Hey Jack! The Worry Monsters
By Sally Rippin

Hey Jack! The New Friend
By Sally Rippin

Hey Jack! The Worst Sleepover
By Sally Rippin

Hey Jack! The Circus Lesson
By Sally Rippin

Hey Jack! The Bumpy Ride
By Sally Rippin

Hey Jack! The Top Team
By Sally Rippin

Hey Jack! The Playground Problem
By Sally Rippin

Hey Jack! The Best Party Ever
By Sally Rippin

Hey Jack! The Bravest Kid
By Sally Rippin

Hey Jack! The Big Adventure
By Sally Rippin

Hey Jack! The Toy Sale
By Sally Rippin

Hey Jack! The Star of the Week
By Sally Rippin

Hey Jack! The Extra-special Group
By Sally Rippin

Hey Jack! The Other Teacher
By Sally Rippin

Hey Jack! The Party Invite
By Sally Rippin

Hey Jack! The Lost Reindeer
By Sally Rippin